Playing Together

BY MICHÈLE DUFRESNE

Pioneer Valley Educational Press, Inc.

Bella is in the basket.
Rosie is in the basket, too.

Bella is in the box.

Rosie is in the box, too.

Bella is in the leaves.
Rosie is in the leaves, too.

Bella is in the water.
Rosie is in the water, too.

Bella is in the mud.
Rosie is in the mud, too.

Bella is in the tub.

Rosie is in the tub, too.